THERE'S AN ALIEN IN MY LUNCHBOX!

Tessa Gearing   **Chris Jevons**

ANDERSEN PRESS

For Jane and Bob. – T.G.

For Noah. – C.J.

First published in Great Britain in 2023 by Andersen Press Ltd.,

20 Vauxhall Bridge Road, London, SW1V 2SA, UK • Vijverlaan 48, 3062 HL Rotterdam, Nederland

Text copyright © Tessa Gearing 2023. Illustration copyright © Chris Jevons 2023.

The rights of Tessa Gearing and Chris Jevons to be identified as the author and illustrator of this

work have been asserted by them in accordance with the Copyright, Designs and Patents Act, 1988.

1 3 5 7 9 10 8 6 4 2

British Library Cataloguing in Publication Data available.

ISBN 978 1 83913 168 4

I brought my favourite **storybook** to school for Show and Tell. But characters keep **jumping out** ... this isn't going well.

There's an **alien** in **my** lunchbox!
He's **eaten** all my **grapes**.
I bet he eats my sandwich next,
but what if he **ESCAPES?**

There's a **witch** in my PE bag.
She's had **A LOT** of fun.

She's tied up all my shoelaces.
I can't get them **undone!**

A **goblin's** sitting at my desk.
She's messed up all my work . . .

and now she's splashing paint around.
My teacher's gone **BERSERK!**

A **ghost's** stuck in the toilets.
He's made an awful **stink.**
And all his ghastly burps and slime
have gone and **blocked the sink.**

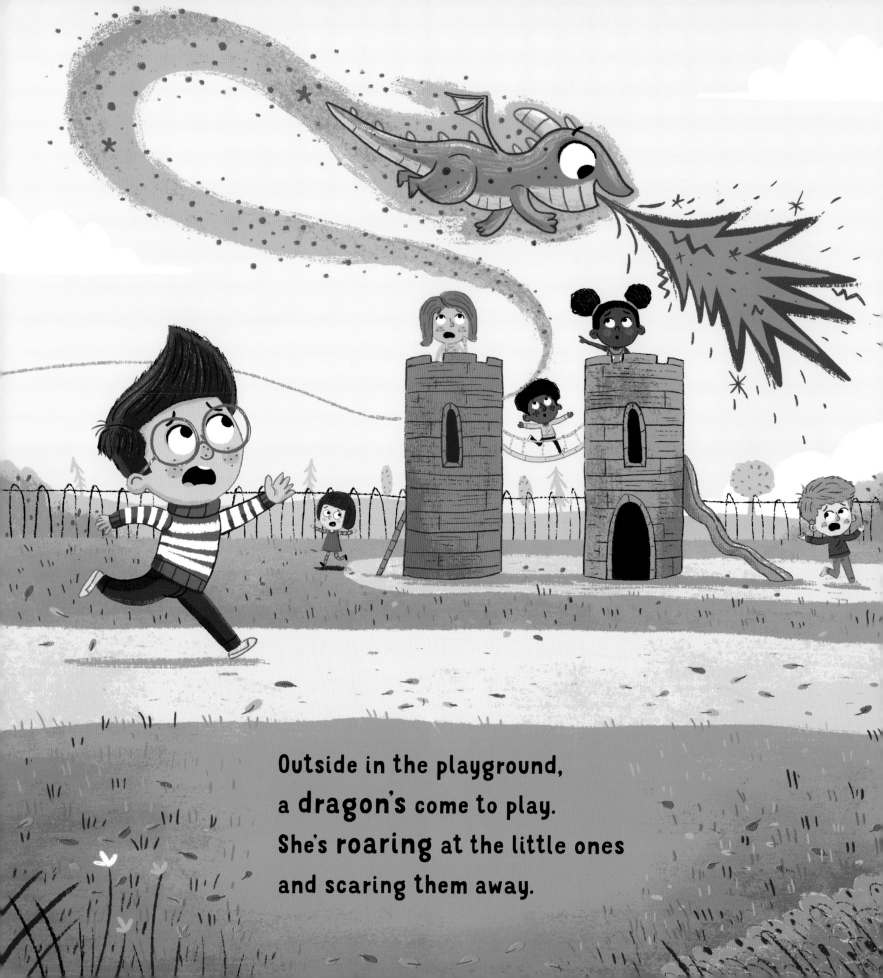

Outside in the playground,
a **dragon's** come to play.
She's **roaring** at the little ones
and scaring them away.

These creatures are so **troublesome**!
They're hiding in the queue.
I'm going to have to find them all –
and **catch them** quickly too!

The teacher calls out:
"**In you come!**

Put everything away."
We start to make a circle,
it's our quiet time of day.

He says, "Now fetch your storybook
to show to everyone."
But with no characters inside,
this won't be too much fun.

As all my classmates settle down,
I rush around the room.
What is that **whizzing** past my head?
It's **Witch** – she's on her broom!
I chase her to the playhouse roof.

She's trapped – she has to stop!

Grabbing **Dragon** by her tail,
I **stuff** her down my top.

Teacher's lost his glasses
so there's some
time to spare . . .

I think I've
spotted Goblin –
she's stuck in
Nita's hair.

Untangling her is difficult.
She's wriggling and squealing . . .

And **Ghost** will be impossible –

he's floating by the ceiling!

Now **Ghost**, where are you hiding?
I hear a "WooOOOOOoo!" noise.
It's coming from the wooden box
where we keep all our toys.

I see the teacher coming back.
The characters are waving!
I slip them back inside the book
and hiss: "Stop misbehaving!"

At last we have our Show and Tell.
I open up my book.
Are all the creatures ready?
I can hardly bear to look.

But all of them are BRILLIANT!
Ghost twirls, dragon wiggles.
And the final illustration . . .

Makes us all collapse in giggles!

The book's safe in my backpack
for hometime in the hall.
The characters are fast asleep . . .

I'm glad I caught them all!